For more than forty years,
Yearling has been the leading name
in classic and award-winning literature
for young readers.

Yearling books feature children's
favorite authors and characters,
providing dynamic stories of adventure,
humor, history, mystery, and fantasy.

Trust Yearling paperbacks to entertain,
inspire, and promote the love of reading
in all children.

SHREDDERMAN

meet the
GECKO

BY: WeNDeLiN VaN DRaaNeN

ILLUSTRATED bY: BRIAN BIGGS

A YEARLING BOOK

WeNDeLiN VaN DRaaNeN

For my shredder-nephews, Bryan, Jefferson, and Kyle.

And special thanks to Leslie Parsons for her help with research.

BRIAN BIGGS

For Cheryl and Michael, who never told me

not to draw on things.

Published by Yearling, an imprint of Random House Children's Books
a division of Random House, Inc., New York

Visit us on the Web! www.randomhouse.com/kids

Educators and librarians, for a variety of teaching tools,
visit us at www.randomhouse.com/teachers

ISBN-13: 978-0-440-41914-3
ISBN-10: 0-440-41914-X

Reprinted by arrangement with Alfred A. Knopf Books for Young Readers

Printed in the United States of America

September 2006

10

OPM

CONTENTS

CHAPTER 1
Big News

I was in the middle of updating my Shredderman Web site when Dad barged through my bedroom door.

"Nolan!"

I shot straight up, banging my knee against the desk. "Da-ad!" I spun to face him. "Dad, you're supposed to knock!"

A month ago this would have been a mammoth problem. A month ago Mom and Dad didn't know that Shredderman—Cedar Valley's very own cyber-superhero—was just an ordinary fifth grader.

Me!

But my parents had discovered my secret

identity, which turned out to be okay. They *liked* having a cyber-superhero son. So Dad barging into my room as I was working on my secret Shredderman site wasn't a problem.

It was just painful.

I rubbed my knee. "You know—K-N-O-C-K?"

"I know, I know," Dad said. His head was bobbing like it was on the end of a big, boingy spring. He stepped outside my room and started making big knocking motions on the signs taped to my door.

DO NOT DISTURB!

Knock-knock-knock.

KNOCK!

Knock-knock-knock.

Shhhh...CONCENTRATING!

Knock-knock-knock.

Sometimes parents can be so annoying. I rolled my eyes and called, "Come in!"

Dad charged back in and sat on my bed.

His eyes were big.

His smile was practically cutting his face in two.

And he was bouncing.

Bouncing.

"You'll never guess what," he whispered.

I had to laugh. "What?"

Boingy-boingy-boingy. He grinned. "I couldn't have come up with a better birthday present for you if I'd tried."

"Stop!" I put up my hand. "I hate it when you tell me what my present is. It ruins everything!"

He froze, mid-bounce. "Even if that's how you get exactly what you want?"

"Yes! I'd way rather be surprised."

"Oh," he said, then started bouncing again. "Well, this isn't exactly your birthday *present*. It just happens to be happening on your birthday."

"Da-ad!"

"Ready for a hint?"

"No!"

He picked up Sticky, my giant stuffed gecko, and shook it at me, saying, "Ay cha-wow-wow."

"Da-ad!"

He bounced about two feet in the air, laughing like a madman. Then he whipped his sunglasses out of his pocket and put them on Sticky. "Hey, *hombre*," he said in the worst Mexican accent ever, "Aaay'm comeeeeeng to your town. How would you like to meeeeeet me?"

"Da-ad! What are you *talking* about?" And then every hair on my body shot straight out. "Do you...? You don't...I mean, they can't..."

Boingy-boingy-boingy, went my dad and Sticky on my bed. "Oh, yes they can, and they are!"

"But why? *When?*"

"That's my boy, asking the who, what, when, where, and why! A chip off the old block. A reporter's reporter! A fellow investigator! A man after my own—"

"Da-ad!"

"Sorry, champ. Sorry." He cleared his throat and said, "The whole cast and crew of *The Gecko and Sticky* are coming into town to film back-to-

5

back episodes. They think Cedar Valley's Old Town will make the perfect setting and have rented the entire Historian Hotel for four days. And because I'm the *Gazette*'s number one reporter, I get to cover the event!"

"Wow!"

"*And,*" he said, leaning in, "I've arranged an interview with 'The Gecko.'"

"Really?"

"Uh-huh. On your birthday."

"And I...I get to come along?"

"That's right! I told their publicity coordinator that it was your birthday and that you were a huge fan. She said, 'By all means, bring him along.'"

My jaw was dangling.

My eyes were bulging.

I looked at the giant *The Gecko and Sticky* poster on my wall and whispered, "I get to meet The Gecko?"

He put my super-sized Sticky aside and said, "Well, you get to meet Chase Morton, the boy who *plays* The Gecko."

"Oh...oh, right." I was still staring at the poster of him—blue jeans, T-shirt, baseball cap, shades—he was the coolest superhero ever. He didn't need some funny disguise. The Gecko was a regular kid just like me, only older.

Which had taken my parents forever to catch

on to. I'd been watching the show for at least six months when my mom asked, "The Gecko's the *boy*? I thought The Gecko was the *lizard*."

She was having this revelation in the middle of a really great episode.

"That's right," I whispered, hoping she'd get the hint.

"But . . . why isn't the boy named Sticky and the gecko named The Gecko?"

"Mo-om!"

"I'm serious, Nolan! I don't understand this at all!"

I said really fast, "Sticky's named Sticky because he's a kleptomaniac. He steals stuff like crazy!"

"But I thought he was a *good* gecko."

"He *is*. He's just got a bad habit."

"But—"

"Mo-om! I'm trying to listen!"

"Okay, okay! I'll talk to you later."

When she and Dad finally figured it out, they became fans, too.

Especially of Sticky.

You just can't help it!

"And Sticky," my dad was saying as I stared at the poster, "well, I imagine he's largely computer-animated. I mean, there's no such thing as a talking gecko lizard, right?"

I looked at Sticky, grinning away on The Gecko's shoulder. I knew he wasn't real, but he sure seemed real on TV. And yeah, The Gecko's the superhero—he's the one with the magic Aztec wristband that gives him powers. Like walking up walls, or disappearing, or super-strength...that sort of thing. But Sticky's the one who found the power-band and gave it to him in the first place. He's the one who's funny and sassy and *smart*. It's easy to forget he's just...animated. Or a robot. Or...

"Nolan?" Dad waved a hand in front of my face.

"Huh? Oh! Oh, right." I scratched my head. "Computer-animated. Of course. Cool."

After all, I love computers, right? Computer animation is *totally* cool.

Dad seemed a little concerned. "You okay, champ?"

"I'm great! This is so, so cool!"

"*Sí, señor,*" my dad said, ruffling my hair. "The Gecko and Sticky meet Shredderman."

My eyes got big.

My heart started racing.

"You didn't tell them, did you?"

"'Course not! It's top-secret, I know that."

I let out a deep breath. It was weird enough that my parents and teacher knew I was Shredderman. No way did I want a kleptomaniacal lizard to find out!

Or The Gecko.

After all, they were superheroes on TV.

I was one in real life.

CHAPTER 2
Impossible!

Bubba Bixby is someone I don't talk to if I can help it. He's big. He's mean. He's got breath like moldy onions, and believe me, he's not afraid to use it.

Bubba used to make fun of everyone and everything. Then I turned into Shredderman. I caught him in the act of bullying. And stealing. I posted his crimes, and his big butt, on the World Wide Web and challenged him to change his ways or pay.

My teacher, Mr. Green, says it's been a partial success. He says all the teachers watch Bubba more closely. He says Bubba *is* showing signs of maturing, and that if we keep working at it, someday we'll find the key to his kindness.

Ha! No matter what I do, Bubba still calls me Nerd.

Bubba still steals stuff.

Bubba still lies.

Which is why **Bubba's Big Butt** is still on the World Wide Web. It's the only revenge I've got, and as long as he's a jerk, that's where it's staying.

Then the day before my birthday, I saw Bubba at school and barely recognized him.

He was *smiling*.

Bubba has lots of teeth. Dirty, fangy teeth. And when he smiles, it's more like a big dog snarling. So normally when Bubba Bixby smiles, kids run.

But this smile was different.

It was . . . *happy?*

He was talking to his friends, Max and Kevin, acting like he'd just found a million bucks. His hands were waving in the air. His eyebrows were flying up and down.

His *ears* looked like they were trying to flap!

I wasn't the only one who noticed it. Kids all over the playground were staring. They were circling around him, a safe distance away. Nobody knew what to think.

Nobody had ever seen Bubba Bixby look like this before.

Then I heard Ian McCoy say to his friend Vinnie, "Wow... is that weird, or what?"

I did a few steps of my power-walk until I was right next to Ian. "What do you think's going on?" I asked him.

"Gotta be really diabolical," Ian whispered.

"Yeah," Vinnie added. "Maybe even deadly."

"Whatever he's planning," Ian said, "I hope I'm not on the receiving end of it."

Then Vinnie snapped his fingers and said, "Hey! Maybe he's figured out who Shredderman is."

Uh-double-oh! I tried to act cool as I asked, "You... you think so?"

"Yeah!" Ian whispered. "That must be it! What else would make the Bubmeister *that* excited?"

Ian and Vinnie walked off, leaving me to sweat bullets alone. What if they were right?

What if he'd figured it out?

What if this was my last day on planet Earth?

I watched Bubba a little while longer, then decided that there was only one way to find out.

I took a deep breath.

I snugged down the straps of my backpack.

Then I walked right up to Bubba and his friends and said, "Hi, guys," pretending I was cool as dry ice. "What's going on?"

Bubba stared at me. "Who's this guy?" he said to the other two, pretending that he'd never seen me before.

"Dunno," Max said. "But he sure looks like a..."

"*Nerd!*" they all cried together, then started laughing.

I'd never been so happy to be called a nerd in my whole life. It meant they didn't know! They didn't have any *idea* I was Shredderman.

I let out the breath I'd been holding and started talking really fast. "Hey, you don't have to call me names. You were just looking pretty excited, that's all. I thought it might be something, you know, great. Fantastic. Amazing! Maybe even awesome! Astounding! Or...or out of this world!"

Wow, I was a regular yapping machine.

Bubba thought so, too. "Shut up, Nerd."

"Yeah," Kevin added. "You sound like a stupid thesaurus."

Both of Bubba's eyebrows shot up at Kevin. "Thesaurus? *Thesaurus?*" He hitched a thumb my way. "You sound like *him,* dork."

Max said, "Kevvy was just tryin' to explain things in a way the nerd would understand."

Kevin nodded like crazy, saying, "Honest! I ain't never even *touched* a thesaurus!"

Bubba shrank back down to Godzilla size and snorted, "Good thing." Then he turned to me and said, "Now scram! You're ruining my good mood."

So believe me, I started power-walking out of there. But then I overheard Kevin say to Bubba, "So go on. I want to hear more about meeting The Gecko."

I came skidding to a halt and froze for a whole nanosecond. Then I threw my power-walk in reverse and asked, "Did you say you're going to meet The Gecko?"

"I said, scram!" Bubba shouted.

"Yeah!" Kevin added. "Scram, Nerd!"

"But...but...are you really going to meet The Gecko? How?" A crazy part of me wanted to tell them that *I* was going to meet him the next day. For my birthday!

Max leaned at me and said, "He'll figure out a way, Nerd. He's, like, his number one fan!"

I almost said, No, he's not! but then they all shouted, "Scram!" so I zoomed out of there.

But still, I couldn't believe it. This was impossible!

Or, at least, the weirdest thing since the discovery of quarks!

Bubba Bixby and I had something in common.

CHAPTER 3
Secret Knock

I've never had a big party for my birthday. My mom tried to make me have one last year, but I couldn't figure out who to invite. Trinity Althoffer is the only person who's halfway nice to me, but she's a girl. Besides, she's into horses, not computers. Or math. Or science.

Now that I think about it, I have more in common with Bubba Bixby.

Scary!

My parents always give me a really great present for my birthday, though. That's how I got my digital camera.

And my scanner.

And my bike!

They always take me someplace cool, too. Like bowling, or to an arcade, and once even to a theme park. I love roller coasters!

All those lateral G's.

Vertical G's!

Think about the science involved!

Roller coasters employ gravity, centrifugal force, momentum, and acceleration.

They're amazing!

The wildest roller coaster I've ever been on had five loop-de-loops and seven in-line twists. I thought for sure I was going to die!

My head was dizzy!

My body was shaking!

My stomach kept flying up in my ears!

But it turns out twelve inversions on a roller coaster was nothing compared to meeting The Gecko.

My stomach was so topsy-turvy I thought for sure I was gonna barf!

And that was *before* my dad picked me up at school.

I didn't tell anyone at school where I was going. I was dying to, but now that I knew that Bubba wanted to meet The Gecko, it was way too dangerous to talk about!

If Bubba found out, he would want to pound me! The only person I could have told was Mr. Green, but he was in Oregon, visiting his brother, who was having a heart operation. So I kept my mouth zipped at school, but it was hard! And when the release slip came from the office and our substitute, Miss Newby, told me I could go, I tripped over my feet and my seat and molecules of thin air racing out of there.

My whole body felt like it was going to burst!

On the drive over, my dad let me sit up front with him. I wouldn't exactly call it sitting, though. It was my turn to bounce around!

As we got near Old Town, Dad said, "Hey,

champ. Take a deep breath, okay? He's just a *guy*."

I tried, but my lungs were closed up tight.

"You've got your camera, right?"

I nodded.

"And your poster for him to sign?"

I nodded some more.

"So, relax. He'll like you fine." He tousled my hair. "How could he not? You're a superhero, just like him!"

"Da-ad!"

He just laughed.

Cedar Valley has one fancy hotel, and that's where The Gecko was staying. The hotel's called the Historian, and it's part of a bunch of buildings that make up Old Town Square. Not that the Square is really a square, which has always kind of bugged me. It's more a U.

Mom says I shouldn't take things so literally.

Dad says I should look at the park area in the middle of the U because *it's* a square.

I say they should quit calling it something it's not.

Or build a fourth side.

Anyway, all the buildings in Old Town are wooden and connected with a big, wide, creaky walkway. The Historian is wooden, too, only it sticks way up in the sky. It's seven stories tall!

As we drove past, we could see people setting things up outside the hotel. There was a giant scissor crane!

Rolling dollies!

Big silver reflectors!

Lights!

Cameras!

Pretty soon there would be *action*.

I was looking all around for The Gecko. Was he there?

Dad was leaning across me, looking out my window, too. "Do you see him?"

"Not yet. Do you?"

"Nope. Looks like they're still setting up. I think he comes out when they're all ready to shoot."

The car behind us honked. We were stopped in the middle of the street! And since you're not allowed to park cars in front of Old Town, we drove around the corner to the parking lot. A whole section of it was blocked off for semi-trucks and moving vans and trailers and limos.

The place was packed!

"What's all that?" I asked.

"Movie equipment, I suppose. And trailers for the stars, maybe." He smiled at me. "I'm just guessing, Nolan. This is a first for me, too."

"Wow...." I hung my head out the window and looked ahead as Dad got closer. "Do you think The Gecko's in one of those trailers?"

"Maybe so. But I was told to go to the hotel, so that's what we're going to do."

After Dad parked the car, we walked into Old Town and cut across the park. We watched people setting up equipment outside the Historian for a few minutes, and then Dad said, "We'd better get going, Nolan. I don't want to be late."

I'd never been inside the Historian, but I had gawked through the window plenty of times. They have a giant stuffed grizzly bear inside. It's fierce! It has beady eyes. Huge yellow teeth. Even bigger claws! And it's standing on its hind legs, roaring.

Now that I think about it, it looks an awful lot like Bubba.

When we went inside the hotel, I discovered that the grizzly bear had company. There's a stuffed buffalo, an elk, a deer, a boar, and a bighorn sheep! There are also wagon wheels and gold-mining pans and blacksmithing tools. And the walls are covered with maps. Cool X-Marks-the-Spot kind of maps!

We crossed through the lobby, going under ceiling lights that were made out of antlers. Off to one side, there were swinging saloon doors, and to the right was a big, swooping staircase.

We walked up to a long wooden counter, and a man on the other side said, "May I help you?"

"Yes," my dad said. "I'm Steven Byrd. I have an appointment to see Chase Morton."

"Very good," the man said, and picked up a phone.

When he hung up, he pointed behind us and said, "If you'll wait in the green room, someone will be right down."

The green room was not green, it was tan. But it had lots of food on long tables that were arranged in the shape of an L. The tablecloths were bright white and went clear to the floor, and on top were big black vases with pine branches and pinecones sticking out.

"Why did he call it a green room, Dad?"

"That's just what they call a hospitality room, champ. I'm not sure why."

Dad spotted a big steel coffee urn.

I spotted a big stack of cookies.

Peanut butter!

Yum!

After a little while, a lady with red hair came in and said, "Steven Byrd?"

Dad said, "That's me."

The lady put her hand out to Dad and said, "I'm Henna Blockwell. We spoke on the phone?"

Dad shook her hand and smiled. "A pleasure to meet you. This is my son, Nolan."

"Well, hello, Nolan," she said. "I hear you're a fan of the show."

I gulped.

I nodded.

My tongue tried to dive down my throat.

She chuckled, then said, "Well, come on up. Chase wants to conduct the interview in his suite."

We rode the elevator up. I watched the floor numbers light as we were boosted higher and higher: 2, 3, 4, 5, 6, 7, *ding*. Top floor!

The doors clanged back and we followed Henna Blockwell down the hall. We turned a corner and went down another hall. And another! The doors started having numbers *and* names.

Room 724 was named *Wagon Wheel*.

Room 727 was *Gold Nugget*.

Room 730 was *Prospector's Dream*.

And the very last door, where we stopped— Room 733—was *Eureka!*

The Henna lady did a secret knock at the door. She did it soft. She did it quick! But I recognized it as an easy mathematical progression—3-2-1.

I knew The Gecko's secret knock!

Then we heard a voice call, "Come in!"

It was time to meet The Gecko!

CHAPTER 4
Meeting The Gecko

It was dark in The Gecko's room.

And cold!

The Henna lady said, "Chase, this is Mr. Byrd, the reporter from the *Cedar Valley Gazette*. And this is his son, Nolan. Nolan's the boy who's having a birthday today, remember?"

"Cool," The Gecko said, but he didn't even look up. He was sitting cross-legged on his bed, his thumbs attacking the buttons of a PlayStation controller.

I checked him out for a minute. He looked just like he does on TV!

Then I checked out the television that was sitting on a big wooden cabinet in front of him.

"Tekken 3?" I asked. "I love that game! It may be old, but it's still my favorite!"

"You have it at home?" He still didn't take his eyes off the TV. He was too busy whaling on his opponent with flying kicks.

"Nah. My parents won't get me a PlayStation."

He took a split second to look at me. "That's cold!"

I didn't want to embarrass my dad, so I said, "It's all right." I watched him battle and said, "Yoshimitsu is my favorite character, too."

"Gunjack's better on blocking. And the way True Ogre breathes fire is way cool—"

"But Yoshimitsu's got the deathcopter trick! And he can do backflips. I love backflips."

"Backflips?" he asked. "How do you make him do backflips?"

I almost said, You don't know how to do backflips? but I caught myself in the nick of time. Instead, I said, "You tap the Back button three times, really fast."

He tried it, but it didn't work. "How?" he asked, and handed over the controller.

"Like this, see?" I said, and tapped the button until Yoshimitsu started doing backflips.

"Wow!"

I handed the controller back and The Gecko sent Yoshimitsu backflipping like crazy. "Now try the deathcopter trick!" I told him. "Before Gunjack gets you!"

"Hoo-hoo-hoo!" he laughed, making Yoshimitsu's sword spin like a helicopter blade. He flew Yoshimitsu out of danger and whaled on Gunjack on his way down.

"I won!" he cried. "That was way cool!"

Henna Blockwell cleared her throat and said, "Chase? You're scheduled to give Mr. Byrd an interview. And we do have to get it done before they call for you."

"Aw, Henna," he said. Then he jumped up and got a second controller from behind the TV. "Let me play the kid one game, okay?" He grinned at me and said, "It is his *birth*day, right?"

Henna looked at him, then me, then Dad.

Dad smiled and said, "I don't mind. And it would absolutely make Nolan's day."

She sighed and said, "One game, Chase. One. You're on a pretty tight schedule today."

In all my wildest dreams, I never could have pictured it.

Me sitting next to The Gecko.

Battling him in Tekken 3.

Beating him in Tekken 3!

This was the best birthday ever!

Before the second battle, I showed him some tricks. He still didn't beat me. So on the third game I held back.

I didn't want him to be mad at me!

After the third game, Henna turned off the TV and said, "Come on, boys. Time to get to work."

"You're good!" The Gecko said to me. "And you don't even have a PlayStation?"

I shrugged. "Dad and Mom take me to Mother Lode's Pizza sometimes. They've got a Tekken 3 game there."

"Still." He faced Dad and said, "Cool kid you've got here."

Cool? The Gecko thought *I* was cool?

Wow.

"Thanks," my dad said. And boy, was he smiling!

"So, fire away," The Gecko said. "What do you want to know?"

Henna glanced at her watch and said softly, "I have to check on a few things. I'll be back in twenty minutes, Chase."

When she was gone, Dad opened his notebook and said, "So. What's your impression of Cedar Valley so far?"

The Gecko shrugged. "Pretty cool, I guess. Small."

Dad nodded.

"Cool trees. Cool town square." He grinned at me. "Cool kids." He moved over to a couch and kind of sprawled out. "Truth is, I've mostly just been learning my lines. I hate going out."

"Why's that?" Dad asked.

"'Cause every time I go out, some jerk sticks a camera in my face. Next thing you know, I'm on

36

the pages of the *Star Gazer* or *Idol Watch* with some insane story about how I'm a criminal, or an idiot, or an *alien* or something."

"Really?" I asked.

"Yeah, really. Like, one time they caught me stretching and yawning at a restaurant, and the next thing I know they've got me in the paper with the headline 'Teen Heartthrob Goes Berserk.' The story said I thrashed around, destroying things in the restaurant."

"No way!"

He laughed. "Oh, way. One time it was 'Gecko Tortures Turtles!' I was just, you know, animating this little kid's turtle for him, but they made it look like I was tearing the turtle's arms off. The next day all these animal rights activists showed up at our location with picket signs. I told them I hadn't tortured any turtles, but they just got more pictures of me and made up more lies. One time they even had my head attached to a big sumo

body with some total-lie story about how I was killing myself with candy bars."

"Wow," I said. "I can't believe they get away with that."

"It's crazy," he said. "There's one guy in particular that's, like, *obsessed* with following me around."

"A reporter?" Dad asked.

"Yeah. Some jerk named Joel Bowl."

"Joel Bowl?" Dad said. "That can't possibly be his real name."

"It is, believe it or not. But everyone calls him Joel the Mole, or just the Mole, 'cause the creep looks like one."

"A mole?" I asked.

"Yeah. He'll do anything for a story. He lies and badgers and just gets in your face. He does outrageous stuff, too. Like planting dog poop outside your hotel room so he can get a picture of you stepping in it and grossing out. Or he'll climb up to your window so he can take pictures of you in your boxers. You name it, he's willing to do it."

"That's unbelievable," my dad said.

"That's nothing. He does illegal stuff, too. *Criminal* stuff. Like starting fires or breaking and entering or..." He shook his head. "Like I said, he's done it all."

"Sue him!" I cried.

The Gecko laughed. "Believe me, I've tried. And lots of people *have* sued him. But he's still out there making up lies. No one can actually ever *pin* anything on him." He turned to my dad and said, "Anyway, we should get back to the interview, or Henna will be all over my case."

So Dad ran down a bunch of questions. *Boring* questions. Like about where he grew up, how he liked being a celebrity, what he did in his free time, did he have a tutor for school, did he see himself as a role model, what advice would he give to kids.... He didn't ask a thing about being a superhero. Or life with a talking gecko. Or what he would do if the *real* Damien Black ever had him in his clutches.

Boy. Did my dad have a lot to learn about interviewing superheroes!

Then before we knew it, Henna was back, telling Chase he had to get to the makeup trailer.

"May I take a picture of Chase and Nolan?" my dad asked. "And Nolan brought a poster for an autograph. I hope you don't mind."

"Not a bit," Chase said. And while I hurried to get my digital camera and poster out of my backpack, he laughed and added, "Just don't sell it to Joel the Mole."

"No way!" I said.

He signed my poster, then put his hand on my shoulder while Dad took aim with my camera and said, "Say cheese!"

"Nah," Chase said. "Say, Buy a PlayStation!"

We both laughed, and Dad clicked. And after we said a million thank-yous, Dad and I left.

But the second we stepped outside the door, a round-bellied man with greasy black hair jumped out from behind a big plant and, *wreeenga-wreeenga-wreeenga*, he shot me with a gigantic camera.

Before we knew what had hit us, the guy said,

"Blast!" in a high, whiny voice, then wrinkled his pointy nose and scurried away through the stairwell door.

CHAPTER 5
Joel the Mole

"Joel the Mole!" Dad and I cried together.

"We have to warn The Gecko!" I said.

"You mean Chase," my dad corrected.

I started to knock on his door regular, then remembered—I knew the secret knock!

Knock-knock-knock!

Knock-knock!

Knock!

Henna answered the door and looked pretty surprised to see me.

"Joel the Mole! He's here!" I cried. "He was hiding behind that plant! He jumped out and took a picture of me, then ran down those stairs!"

"What?" Chase was at the door now, too. "He's *here?*"

"What did he look like?" Henna asked.

"Like a mole! Kinda fat. Kinda oily. Black hair. A twitchy, pointy nose. And long teeth. Long *buck*teeth!"

Chase frowned at Henna. "I *told* you he'd come!"

"Excuse us, won't you please?" Henna said. And while she closed the door in our faces, Chase called, "You're all right, Nolan! I owe ya!"

I couldn't help smiling from ear to ear. The Gecko didn't think I was a nerd. He thought I was all right!

"Well, champ," my dad said. "It's been a pretty exciting day, wouldn't you say?"

He was steering me toward the elevator, but I didn't want to go that way.

I wanted to follow the Mole!

"Hey!" I said, breaking free. "I've got a great

44

idea! Why don't *you* go down the elevator while *I* go down the stairs. Let's see if we can find him!"

"Uh..."

"If you see him, follow him! I'll do the same. I'll meet you in the lobby."

"Uh, I don't know..."

I had already dug out my camera and was heading for the stairwell door.

"Now hold your horses, Nolan."

I shot him a look, and he read it loud and clear: Don't mess with a superhero in pursuit of truth and justice!

But just to make him feel better, I added, "I'm eleven now, Dad. Don't worry!" Then I ducked through the stairwell door.

All of a sudden, I felt like I was inside an old mine shaft going down, down, down.

My eyes were cranked.

My ears were perked.

I was feather-footed!

Fast!

Smooth.

Something about the pursuit of truth and justice makes me do things I normally can't do.

The Mole wasn't in the stairwell. And when I

got to the bottom floor and opened the last door, I could see an EXIT sign to my left and the lobby to my right.

Dad spotted me from over by the elevators and waved. I could tell that he hadn't seen the Mole, either, but I wasn't ready to give up yet! I signaled my dad to go outside through the front door while I went out the side exit. He frowned and shook his head.

Obviously he had a lot to learn about pursuing truth and justice.

I frowned right back and nodded, which made him roll his eyes and sigh, but he headed for the front door.

Yeah!

I snuck outside.

I hid behind bushes.

I darted from tree to tree.

But the Mole was nowhere to be found.

Nowhere!

I saw my dad heading my way, and I thought for sure he'd make me forget about finding the Mole. But then he slowed down.

His eyes sharpened on a big bush.

I looked where he was looking, but didn't see a thing.

Very slyly, he signaled me to stay put. Then he moved his index finger like he was taking a picture.

I ducked behind a tree.

I got my camera ready.

Then Dad cut across the grass and waved his arms through the air, yelling, "Hey! What are you doing back there? There's no loitering allowed here! Get out of here! Go! Go-go-go!"

A big bush shook.

The Mole came out from behind it!

He ran across the grass, getting away from Dad as fast as he could!

And in his hurry to get away from my dad, the

Mole didn't notice me, hiding behind a tree trunk.

Didn't hear my camera activate as he looked over his shoulder at Dad.

Didn't have any idea that he was now one digitally trapped Mole.

CHAPTER 6
Time to Slime!

I didn't want to go back to school.

Didn't want to meet Mom for lunch.

Didn't want to open my birthday presents.

I had work to do!

"Please, Dad? Please-please-please?"

Dad frowned. He moved his mouth from one side to the other. He looked at me with one eyebrow up. Finally he flipped open his cell phone and called Mom.

He whispered a lot.

He said, "Uh-huh" a lot.

He shook his head a lot.

I didn't know what to think!

When he hung up, he said, "Well, champ...

your mother and I have decided that since it *is* your birthday and since you *are* a superhero..."

"Yes-yes-yes!" I cried. "You're the best!"

He started the car and said, "I'll just write my 'Cool Kid Celebrity Visits Cedar Valley' article at home."

The second we were home, I tore down to my room, turned on the computer, and got to work.

USB cable connected—check!

Images of the Mole loaded—check!

Images transferred into Photoshop—check!

This was gonna be fun!

I connected to the Internet and did a search for "Ugly Alien Bodies."

I got half a million hits!

I refined the search. I had to get fewer hits! I tried "Disgusting Alien Bodies."

Only a few thousand hits.

Still too many to sift through, though. So I tried "Weird" + "Disgusting Alien Bodies."

Only a few hundred hits.

Time to take a look!

I scrolled through the first page of Web addresses, and when I saw "Real pictures, Real aliens!" my heart started racing. And when I visited the site and found an image of a huge, slimy green slug dripping with disgusting green pus, I knew I'd found the Mole's new body.

Oh, yeah!

I worked and worked and worked until I got the Mole's face superimposed onto the slug's body. It looked great! Really real!

Next, I added some ugly green arms and put the Mole's camera in between slimy green suction-cup hands.

It was disgusting!

It was vile!

Oh, yeah!

Then I made up a page like you see in those stupid magazines by grocery store checkout stands. I

played around with different fonts and finally picked an old-fashioned typewriter-style one for the headline:

JOEL BOWL EXPOSED!

And under that came the story:

Joel Bowl, the notorious "Mole," was seen yesterday in Cedar Valley, California, where The Gecko and Sticky *is being filmed on location. Members of the entertainment community have long suspected Mr. Bowl to be nothing but an oversized, revolting gastropod, but now proof is at hand. Will the garden community of Cedar Valley tolerate this invasion of slime, stench, and visual horror? Or will this perennial pest be driven away, perhaps once and for all? Stay tuned ... we'll keep you posted.*

Then I put the Slug-Mole picture on the page, added a background of Old Town that I lifted from the Cedar Valley Chamber of Commerce Web site, and presto! I had the Mole just where I wanted him.

Dad popped his head through my door. "How's it going, champ?"

"Great! Come in! You've got to see this!" He hadn't knocked, but who cared?

Dad stood behind me, looking at my computer monitor. He started shaking his head. "How in the world did you *do* that?"

"Piece of cake, Dad."

"Oh, right." He sat down on the edge of my bed, still looking at the monitor. "So now what?"

I gave the page one last save and said, "Now we go do a search."

"For?"

I reopened my Internet connection. "For 'Joel Bowl' plus 'the Mole.'"

"Because?"

"Because that way the search engine will check the entire World Wide Web for any sites that have both *Joel Bowl* and *the Mole* in their text."

"I know, but why are you searching for that?"

"Because . . ." Just then the computer displayed **Web site found** and then *Found: 87 matches for "Joel Bowl" + "the Mole."* "Wa-hoo! Eighty-seven matches!"

"But why?"

I opened up the first site and said, "Because most Web sites have e-mail addresses. I'm going

55

to collect them and send everyone who knows the Mole or hates the Mole a picture of him. I'm going to do to him what he does to other people!"

Dad was starting to nod. "Planning to fight fire with fire?"

I grinned at him and said, "More like give him a taste of his own medicine."

Dad stood up and laughed. "By the time you're done with him, there's no doubt he's going to hate the flavor."

Oh, yeah!

CHAPTER 7
The Mole Tastes His Own Medicine

One of the eighty-seven sites I looked at was for a newspaper in Milwaukee, Wisconsin. Someone there really hated the Mole! There was an article in the archives that cut him down low!

Said he was a liar.

An embarrassment to journalism.

Said his work stank like a sewage line.

They didn't have a picture of him, though.

And they called him Mr. Bowl.

Did they really think that would stop him?

Obviously they didn't have much experience with sneaks and bullies!

I added their e-mail address to the others I'd

collected. They were going to love my slimy Slug-Mole!

There was also a television station in Los Angeles that had "journalist Joel Bowl, known to celebrities as the Mole...," but it was an old link and didn't take me anywhere. I copied and pasted the station's e-mail address, anyway.

You never know.

By the time I'd gone through all the Web sites, I had learned lots about the Mole.

He ruined lives!

People hated him!

He was even worse than The Gecko had told me. He was wicked!

Evil!

A true villain!

Well! Maybe he'd gotten away with it so far, but he'd never gone nose to nose with Shredderman before!

I clicked on Compose.

I put *MOLE ALERT! (Truth and Justice can prevail!)* in the subject line of a new e-mail.

Then I wrote a short note and attached the Slug-Mole page. The note said:

He's a pest! A nuisance! An ugly line of slime across the pages of honest journalism! Lawsuits don't stop him—he oozes out of them. And now we know why! The Mole is really a Slug! Help expose him for who he is! Forward this picture to every journalist, paper, reporter, or celebrity you know! Let's show the world who Joel "the Mole" Bowl really is!

Yours in truth and justice,
Shredderman

I added all the e-mail addresses I found to the To box.

There were a lot!

I spell-checked everything and was in the

middle of giving my mass mailing a final inspection when...

Knock-knock-knock!

I banged my knee.

I spun around.

Mom peeked into my room. "Where's my birthday boy?"

"Mo-om!"

She came in. "Don't you Mo-om me!" She gave me a squeaky smooch on my cheek and said, "I heard you had an outstanding adventure today. Tell me all about it!"

"I have to finish this first."

She squatted next to my chair and looked at the monitor. "Your dad said you were busy shredding on some sleazy reporter. Can I see?"

"Uh..."

"Don't worry! I may not be your sidekick, but I *am* in your corner. Let's see."

So I showed her. And she loved the Slug-

Mole! But when she saw my message and all the people I was sending it to, she started fidgeting.

Her smile turned twitchy.

Her eyes went into hyper-blink.

She said a lot of Uhs and Buts and Do-you-thinks, and finally she just came out and said, "I don't think this is such a good idea, Nolan. I know you've spent all day on it, but I don't want him to *sue* us."

I scowled at her. Fear holds no power over the pursuit of truth and justice!

"Mo-om!"

"I'm serious, Nolan. Let me talk this over with your dad, okay?"

"No!"

Her eyebrows flew to the ceiling.

Her jaw dropped to the floor.

But I held my ground. "He's not going to sue us! He doesn't even know who I am!"

"But—"

"He's a jerk! A liar! He's made up stories about people for years!"

"But—"

"He gets a picture of someone blinking and says they're on drugs! He takes a head and puts it on someone else's body. He photographs people reaching for something and says they're stealing it. You should read all the things I found on the Internet today! People are really hurt by him, and nobody seems to be able to stop him! Even The Gecko's afraid of him! He hides in his room because he's afraid to go out."

"Oh, I don't believe that."

"It's true!"

"But, Nolan—"

I crossed my arms and frowned at her. "You're making me wish I'd never told you I was Shredderman."

She was quiet.

"Mom," I said softly. "I want to stop him. You should want to stop him, too."

"But..."

"Sometimes you have to risk a little in the search for truth and justice."

She looked in my eyes. She looked long and hard.

I didn't blink.

I didn't look away.

I just sat there, steady.

Finally she took a deep breath and eyed my computer monitor. "It's all ready to go?"

I nodded.

She stared at it another minute, then reached over and took my mouse.

I wanted to grab it away from her!

She moved the pointer until it hovered over Send.

What was she doing?

"May I?" she asked me.

Now she *wanted* to send it? But... I looked at the pointer. I looked at her. I'd spent my whole birthday putting this e-mail together—*I* wanted to click on Send. The moment of Send is the grand finale! Just thinking about the information zipping around the world faster than I can blink makes my head float. It's mind-boggling! Astounding!

I *love* clicking the Send button!

But there was my mom, with her hand on my mouse, the pointer hovering over Send.

She had a grin on her face.

She looked like a kid.

A happy kid.

And I could tell that she wasn't doing this just because it was my birthday.

She was doing it because truth and justice were important to her, too.

More important than getting into trouble.

So finally I nodded and said, "Go ahead."

And with that, she clicked, and my *Mole Alert* message flew around the globe.

CHAPTER 8
On the Set!

The next day at school, Bubba was talking about how he'd gone to the *Gecko and Sticky* shoot. How The Gecko had said, "Hey, dude" to him between takes. "I'm going back today," Bubba boasted loud enough for everyone around to hear. "And this time I'm gonna get *on* the set."

"How ya gonna do that?" Kevin asked him.

"I got ways of makin' it happen," Bubba said with a smirk.

Max said, "Can we come, too?"

Bubba squinted at him. "Don't be stupid."

Max shrugged. "Hey, we could, you know, help you get past security or something. You said there was tons of guards and stuff keeping people back."

"Like they're gonna stop *me*?" He looked around at all the kids listening and snorted, "Ha!"

I had come to school dying to tell someone, *any*one, that I had met The Gecko.

That I had gotten his autograph.

That I had a picture of the two of us.

That I had been in his hotel room and played him in Tekken 3!

But after hearing Bubba talk, I felt like I couldn't tell a soul. It would have been like bragging.

And, knowing Bubba, it would have gotten me pounded.

So I sat in class wishing. Wishing that I had a friend I could tell. A friend I could trust. It had been the greatest day of my life, and I couldn't tell anyone about it! I couldn't even tell anyone about the present my parents had given me for my birthday—a high-tech, ultra-lightweight, mega-adjustable, totally cool spy tool.

A collapsible periscope!

I could now spy around doorways!

Over fences!

Maybe I couldn't fly or turn invisible, but with a periscope like this, I could really shred on bad guys!

But that was exactly why I couldn't show it to anyone. The first thing they'd ask would be, "What do you need *that* for?"

It was hard enough being Shredderman and not telling anyone he was me. All the kids at school—well, except Bubba—loved Shredderman. They thought he was cool and funny and smart and...*awesome.*

Me they thought of as a nerd.

If only they could see!

But the fight for truth and justice was bigger than wanting friends.

Bigger than being called Nerd.

Bigger than me.

So keeping my present and my secret identity
to myself wasn't *that* hard. But not being able to
tell any of my classmates that I'd met The Gecko
was torture!

By the end of school, I felt really rotten.

It was no fun having no friends.

No fun at all.

The minute I got home, things changed.

"Nolan! There you are!" my mom cried, getting up from her desk.

Normally my mom's happy to see me, but this was more than that. She was practically busting at the seams. "Guess what?"

"What?"

"Your friend Chase called and invited you to watch them shoot this afternoon."

That word "friend" threw me for a second. "The... The *Gecko* called? *Here?*"

"Well, not exactly. Someone named Henna Blockwell called your father at the *Gazette*. But the point is, Chase Morton thought you were very nice and has invited you to come, you know, hang around backstage...or whatever they call it."

I was standing stock-still, staring at her. Finally I choked out, "Really?"

She laughed and kissed my cheek. "Really! Your father's there already, covering a-day-in-the-life-of-The-Gecko for the *Gazette*, so come on. Do you need a snack before we go?"

I shook my head. I still couldn't seem to blink.

She grabbed a couple of juice pouches anyway, and at the last minute said, "Don't forget your camera! And fresh batteries!"

My mom's the best.

I keep my camera in my backpack. Along with extra batteries, binoculars, string, tape, scissors... and now, one very cool periscope.

So I just took my backpack, and off we went. And by the time we got to Old Town, I'd taken my binder and all my homework books out of it, secured the camera in its special pouch with the secret lens port, and stashed the remote control in my sweatshirt pocket.

My spy-pack was ready!

The cool thing about wearing a spy-pack is that it's like having an eyeball in the back of your head.

No one expects it!

No one suspects it!

And once you figure out how to take pictures backward, it's amazing who you can catch In-The-Act!

I love my spy-pack!

I was testing out my remote control when Mom asked, "Why in the world are you doing all that?"

"Because you never know," I said.

"But I'm sure he'll just let you take pictures of him."

I grinned at her. "But I'm sure the Mole won't."

Her eyebrows went up. "You think he'll be there again?"

"I have a sneaking suspicion."

She shook her head. "You're invited to watch the filming of your favorite show of all time, and you're thinking about the Mole? I just don't get it."

Neither did I, but inside something was telling me to be ready.

Just in case.

CHAPTER 9
And... Action!

After we got our special GUEST badges and cleared security, we were ushered into the hotel. They were getting ready to shoot a scene right in the main lobby!

Mom spotted Dad, who was standing about ten feet behind a camera. We got over to him just as a guy with a patchy little beard called, "Picture's up! Quiet on the set, we're rolling!"

"That's the director," Dad whispered.

"Shhhh!" my mom scolded him.

A lady stuck a clapboard with all sorts of numbers on it in front of a camera, then pulled it away. The director called, "Action!" and suddenly evil Damien Black appeared at the top of the stairs. He snuck down on his tiptoes! His eyes were darting all around! He had on a long coat. Black boots. A twisty mustache. He was holding a long double-bladed ax!

I had the powerful urge to hiss.

Damien Black is sooooo nasty!

The Gecko was around the corner, trying to switch the power ingot in his magic wristband from super-strength to wall-walker. He was trapped! And since the magic wristband only allows for one power at a time, he was in trouble!

"And cut!" the director cried. Then he called, "Live gecko inside Chase's sweatshirt. Let's go!"

I whispered, "This is so cool, Dad! Thank you! Thank-you-thank-you!"

People scurried all around, moving cameras, moving chairs. Chase grinned at me and tossed his head back a little like, Hey! while a lady patted powder on his nose and forehead.

I waved and smiled.

Was I dreaming?

My mother squeezed my arm and smiled at me. "Pretty interesting, isn't it?" she whispered.

I nodded. It was amazing to be on the set of my favorite show.

And very...strange.

Someone gave Chase a gecko.

A gecko? What was I thinking? They gave him Sticky!

The funniest sidekick of all time!

Chase stroked Sticky on the head and talked to him quietly. Sticky looked kind of small. And brown. The real Sticky's orange. With yellow stripes. And sometimes sunglasses!

I took out my binoculars and zoomed in on the two of them. Wow. Sticky might look different, but Chase was really talking to him. And I swear Sticky was talking back! I could practically hear him saying, "*Ay-chihuahua. Eees theees the best you got?*"

Then Chase put Sticky inside his sweatshirt, held on to him, and gave the director a nod.

I kept watching through my binoculars.

77

"Quiet on the set!" the director called. "Close-up on his shoulder. And...action!"

Chase let go of Sticky and put his hand back on his power-band. In a flash, Sticky wriggled out of the sweatshirt and up onto Chase's shoulder. His head moved from side to side, then he sort of jumped on top of Chase's ball cap and looked around.

After a second of Sticky looking around, the director called, "And cut!"

Everyone started talking at once.

Chase was grinning from ear to ear.

The director was, too. "Unbelievable!" he said. "On a first take, too! And that bonus jump on the head! Beautiful! Brilliant! That's what I like from my radical reptiles! Whatever you said to him, Chase, nice work."

Chase was taking Sticky off his hat, still grinning away. "Hey. Just call me the guy who talks to geckos!"

Everyone laughed. Then Mom whispered across me to Dad, "I always thought it was some kind of robot. Or computer animation."

Dad nodded. "They tell me that most of it is computer-generated. They have a toy gecko and a remote-controlled gecko, but they use a live one sometimes, too." He laughed. "They sure couldn't have gotten the remote-controlled one to jump on his head!"

"They must've gotten lucky with that."

Dad nodded. "Oh, very!"

A remote-controlled gecko? Computer-animated? So what if the gecko Chase had wasn't orange. It was still Sticky! I'd just seen him in action! What more proof did people need?

Sticky was real!

I tried to tune my parents out and watched the people who were scurrying around to set up the next scene. Damien Black would be coming down the rest of the stairs. The Gecko would click in the wall-walker ingot at the last minute.

He'd climb up the wall!

He'd...

"How do they make it look like he's climbing walls?" Mom asked Dad.

"Shhhh!" I told her. "He'll have the wall-walker ingot in!"

Mom looked at Dad.

Dad looked at Mom.

They both raised their eyebrows.

"Picture's up!" the director called. Then he said, "Quiet on the set.... And... action!"

Boom! Crash! Clank!

Everyone froze.

I looked around. Was this sound effects?

Thump!

The saloon doors burst open, then closed, then burst open again. But no one came through!

"Let go!" a voice inside the saloon cried. "I just wanna meet The Gecko!"

I couldn't believe my ears. I whispered, "That

sounds like—" but before I could say his name, Bubba Bixby crashed through the door.

"CUT!" the director shouted. "Who's that clown? Get him *out* of here!"

Bubba tried to touch Chase, but before he could, men in black T-shirts were all over him. And as they hauled Bubba away, Bubba reached for The Gecko, saying, "Hey, I just want to shake your hand! I just wanna..." The men muscled Bubba along as he shouted over his shoulder, "Man, I'm your number one fan!"

Everyone was scowling.

The director looked mad!

Bubba's head swept around as he turned to face forward, but then, like in slow motion, his head turned back.

And his eyes stopped.

And locked!

Right on me.

CHAPTER 10
Hot off the Press!

"Wow," my mom whispered. "That boy's gotten big."

"Oh, yeah," I choked out, thinking about how Bubba'd find some way to pound me at school the next day.

"How'd he get in here?" Dad said.

"He's Bubba, Dad. He has ways."

Everyone was just starting to settle down when Chase said, "Has anyone seen Sticky?" He was patting himself all over, looking around.

After a minute of Sticky not showing up, some woman announced, "We've got a gecko on the loose. Come on, people, let's find it."

Everyone looked around.

On the floor.

All around the furniture.

I looked up. Geckos love to climb. They can hang upside down, no problem!

Geckos are way, way cool.

And seeing how this gecko was Sticky, well, he could be anywhere! "They should check the cash register!" I whispered to Dad. "Or the safe!" I grinned and asked him, "You still got your watch?"

Sticky is such a kleptomaniac!

Dad laughed and put his arm on my shoulder. "You are just kidding, right?"

I shrugged and smiled, but part of me really wanted to check the cash register.

Just in case.

Someone probably should have, too, because Sticky didn't show up. Finally the director called, "Get the gecko wrangler! Everyone else, lunch, half hour! We've got miles to go before we sleep."

Most people filed into the tan green room. Some people ran upstairs. I was dying to go over and thank The Gecko for inviting me to watch, but I didn't have to.

He came over to me!

"Hey, Nolan," he said. "Glad you could make it."

"Thanks for inviting me!" I told him.

He turned to Mom and Dad. "Cool kid you got here."

Mom was smiling big. She put out her hand and said, "I'm Eve Byrd, Nolan's mother."

He nodded. "And I'm Chase Morton"—he wiggled his eyebrows my way—"The Gecko!"

Just then Henna Blockwell came over with a paper in her hand and a grin on her face. A grin that didn't seem to really *go* with her face.

It was... *goofy*.

"Chase," she said, then looked around at the rest of us. "Sorry for interrupting, but..." She handed Chase the paper. "This came via fax. Maggie sent it from L.A. You're not going to believe it."

I saw the paper as Henna passed it to Chase.

So did Dad.

And Mom.

Our eyes got big.

We tried to make them stay small.

Tried to act cool.

But our mouths and shoulders and heads were twitching all around. Even as a murky fax copy, there was no mistaking my Slug-Mole!

The Gecko read the article. He was grinning so big I thought his ears would push right off the back of his head! Finally he looked at Henna and said, "Who wrote this?"

"Well, it's David Egbert's column, but obviously his source is a mystery man."

"Yeah," Chase said. "Shredderman."

Henna was still grinning. "It's hilarious. And even funnier when you realize that Egbert's column is syndicated—this piece will be in papers all around the country!"

Chase laughed and kind of danced in place. "This is so cool! This is...brilliant!"

Slick as a semiconductor, my dad asked, "What's this all about?"

Chase handed over the paper, saying,

"Remember the Mole? The guy you warned me about yesterday?"

Dad nodded. "Mr. Bowl?"

Chase snickered. "Yeah. Well, some guy named Shredderman is giving him a dose of his own medicine."

Dad was skimming the article, nodding. "I've heard of this Shredderman character."

"Really?"

Dad passed the paper to me, saying, "He's something of a local hero."

Chase seemed very interested. "Any idea who he is?"

Uh-triple-oh! I hadn't thought about it until now, but who else knew the Mole was in town? Who else would try to expose him?

Bullets started shooting out my sweat glands.

Dad stayed totally cool, though. He shrugged and said, "I'm actually investigating that for the *Gazette*."

"Well, when you find out, would you let me know? You have no idea how many people would want to thank him."

My heart was pounding double-speed as I read the article. It was everything I'd sent in my e-mail, plus the writer's own stories about the Mole.

Henna eased the paper out of my hands and said, "I'm going to make copies and pass them around. This is just too good!"

Chase said, "Great idea!" then grinned at me and said, "We've probably got time for a quick game of Tekken 3. You up for it?"

Henna grabbed him by the arm. "No way! Absolutely no way." She dragged him along, saying, "As a matter of fact, they need you in wardrobe. No more disappearing acts."

Chase pointed to his magic wristband as he grinned at me and wiggled his eyebrows. "See ya later, Nolan!"

I laughed and waved, and when he was gone I followed Mom and Dad to the side so we'd be out of the way. And while they were debating how long we could stay without wearing out our welcome, a man with a bushy brown goatee went by, pushing a cart of food.

He was wearing a white waiter coat.

A black bow tie.

A chef hat.

Glasses.

He looked like a waiter, doing his job.

But behind his glasses, his eyes were shifty.

Beady.

Darting back and forth.

I blinked. He looked sort of . . . familiar.

Then his nose twitched and I knew why.

It was the Mole!

CHAPTER 11
The Mole Returns

I tugged on Dad's arm and whispered, "Look!"

"Huh?" Dad said.

I twitched my nose and pointed again.

"What is—"

"Shhhhh!" I held up a finger, telling him to wait, then started trailing the Mole.

My mom said, "What is Nolan doing?" but my dad held on to her and kept her quiet.

Inside, my dad's got the heart of a superhero.

I followed the Mole into the green room. There were a bunch of people inside! The tables had tons of stuff on them. Big steel dishes with lids. Stacks of plates. Pyramids of cheese!

Before anyone noticed me, I ducked under the

closest table and hid behind the long white tablecloth. I could see the wheels of the Mole's cart
moving across the room. I crawled along, watching that I didn't bang the table's cross braces with
my backpack.

It wasn't easy!

At the end of the first table, I peeked out the
back side.

Nobody there!

I crawled out and around table legs until I was
hidden under the second table.

My heart was banging. My legs felt shaky!
What was the Mole up to?

The wheels of his cart twisted and turned. I
could see the Mole's feet moving back and forth
around the cart. I pulled up a corner of the tablecloth so I could see better, but I was afraid to pull
it up too high. All I could really see were legs!

Then I remembered—my periscope!

I slipped off my backpack. I unzipped it,

quiiiiiiiet as could be. I pulled out my newest spy tool and pushed it up through the space between the tables. Careful...careful...inch by inch!

I saw the back of a steel dish.

Plates.

A black vase.

Pine needles.

And then...people!

Oh, yeah!

I turned the periscope around slowly... slowly....

Sudden movements are easily detected by the human eye!

And then there he was! In my sights! The Mole!

He was looking shifty, all right. Putting food from the rolling tray onto a table. He was doing it slow. Looking around. Looking up.

Up? Had he spotted Sticky? I turned the periscope, but didn't see Sticky anywhere.

The Mole was up to something, I knew that. But what? And when he made his move, what was I going to do? How was I going to catch him in the act?

Hmmmm.

I pulled the periscope down and took my digital camera out of its spy compartment. I held the camera lens up to the eyepiece of the periscope.

Could you take a picture that way?

I decided to try it. I turned the periscope-camera sideways and slipped the eye of the periscope under the tablecloth. I looked through the camera's viewfinder. I spotted someone's shoes, then clicked a picture.

I put the periscope down and looked at the shot.

It worked! I had a picture of feet! Sharp, in-focus feet!

Then someone called, "Let's hit it!" and pretty soon everyone cleared out of the room.

Everyone except me.

And the Mole!

I put the periscope and the camera together, and at the last minute I switched into movie mode. Then up, up, up went the periscope until I found the Mole.

He was moving around fast! I was having trouble tracking him!

He grabbed a chair.

He yanked it across the room.

He whipped his camera from under a metal serving dome on the rolling tray and slung it around his neck!

He went back to the chair and stood on it!

What was I waiting for? Time to start recording!

I caught him looking around. Pulling something out of his waiter coat.

A lighter!

He flicked the lighter wheel and started a flame.

He held it up to the ceiling!

Up to an automatic sprinkler!

Oh, no! He was trying to make them come on!

The sprinklers would ruin everything! They would soak the green room! The lobby! The cameras! The actors! Everything!

I almost shouted, "Stop, villain!" but I didn't. It was more important to get proof!

The ceiling sprinklers sputtered.

They burst on!

Water sprayed everywhere!

I could hear people in the lobby shouting. Squealing! Screaming!

The Mole jumped off the chair and charged into the lobby. *Wreeenga-wreeenga-wreeenga!* I could hear the Mole's camera shoot and wind through the spray.

"Fire!" somebody shouted. "There must be a fire!"

Wreeenga-wreeenga-wreeenga!

"Cover the cameras!"

Wreeenga-wreeenga-wreeenga!

"Shut off the sprinklers!"

Wreeenga-wreeenga-wreeenga!

The place was going crazy!

My dad charged into the green room. "Nolan?" he called.

"Here, Dad!"

He dived under the table with me. "What are you doing?"

I was collapsing the periscope, stuffing every-thing back in my backpack. "The Mole! He started the sprinklers with a lighter! He's out there getting pictures! You've got to stop him!"

"But—"

"Stop him! Get his camera!"

But by the time Dad scrambled out of the room, it was too late.

The Mole had already disappeared.

CHAPTER 12
Back to the Motherboard

We had an argument on the way home. Mom thought I should turn my movie clip over to the police right away. "No way!" I told her. "It'll give away who Shredderman is!"

Dad, who had now spent some time in the superhero trenches, didn't know whose side to be on. "But, Nolan," he said as we drove away from Old Town. "The whole point of being a superhero is to *help* people."

"But, Dad," I said back, "if they know I'm Shredderman, it's all over! I can't help anyone anymore, ever again!"

"He does have a point, Eve," my dad said to my mom.

"But, Steven, that man ruined...who knows what all he ruined! And he's probably on his way back to...wherever he came from. Right now!"

"I know, I know. But I do think we should give it a little more thought, okay?"

Mom frowned.

Dad drove.

I held on tight to my backpack.

When we got home, Mom and Dad went to the kitchen to make dinner. What they were really doing, though, was still arguing about what to do.

I slammed a few plates around the table, scattered some forks and cups, and charged down to my room.

No way was I going to let them unmask me!

I booted up my computer.

I logged on to the Internet.

I clicked on my Web and mail icons.

But in the middle of getting my camera ready, I stopped.

E-mails were being delivered. *Flick, flick, flick, flick, flick!* They were flying in. *Pouring* in. When the screen finally stopped scrolling up new e-mails, the status bar said: **You have 102 new messages.**

Wow!

The subject line of some was **RE: MOLE ALERT!**

Some were replies to forwarded Mole Alerts!

Some were replies to Mole Alerts that had been forwarded three, five, seventeen times!

My Mole Alert had been to New York!

Maine!

Illinois!

North Dakota, Alabama, Oregon!

Mississippi, Texas, Ohio!

Massachusetts, Missouri, Timbuk...tu?

I did a quick search and learned something new: There really is a Timbuktu. It's in West Africa!

Wow. You know you're a bad guy if people hate you in Timbuktu!

And they did. I blazed through enough replies to know that they all said pretty much the same thing: *You rock, Shredderman! Keep it up!*

Oh, yeah!

I could smell dinner cooking. Was that chicken? No time to lose! I downloaded the fire sprinkler clip. I attached it to a new e-mail—one that would go to everyone! I typed *Mole caught in the act* in the subject line, then wrote a short message:

The attached clip is raw footage. There has been no image manipulation. What you see is what Joel "the Mole" Bowl did at a location shoot for The Gecko and Sticky in Cedar Valley today. Damage and expense are still being assessed, and the Mole is still on the loose. Help stop him! Forward this to every journalist you know. Let's put this menace out of business!

Yours in truth and justice,
Shredderman

I was just finishing up when there was a *knock-knock-knock* at my door.

"No!" I called.

The door opened anyway.

"I said no!"

The room went dead quiet. And cold. Mom and Dad were both standing in the doorway.

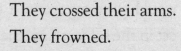

They crossed their arms. They frowned.

Finally my dad said, "We don't appreciate that tone of voice, Nolan."

"But—"

"We'd already decided to let you do what you thought was right," my mom said.

"After all, it *is* your clip," Dad added.

"But—"

"*But,*" my mom interrupted, "we don't ever want to hear you talk to us in that tone of voice again, you hear me? If being Shredderman means you think you can shred on *us*, well, we'll put a stop to this right here and now."

"I ... I'm sorry, Mom," I said. And I was about to say, I thought you were going to try and stop me, only right then something thumped on my knee.

Wiggled up my thigh.

Crossed over my chest!

And faster than you can say Charles Babbage, he was gripping on to my shoulder, looking around the room.

I couldn't believe my eyes.

I was nose to nose with Sticky!

CHAPTER 13
Stowaway Gecko

My mother screamed!

My father held her shoulders and said, "Take it easy, Eve. It's just a gecko."

I grinned at Sticky and said, "Hiya, Sticky. What'cha doin' here?"

"Sticky?" my mom gasped. "That's *Sticky*?"

I looked her way. "Who'd you think it was, Mom?"

"But—"

"He must've stowed away in my backpack!" I was petting him with my index finger. Softly, slowly, back along the top part of his head. I smiled at him, careful not to show my teeth.

"Didn't'cha, boy?"

He looked right at me, and I swear...

He smiled back!

"Uh, Nolan?" my dad whispered. "Don't you think you should catch him?"

"Did you see that, Dad? Did you see that?"

"See what?"

I looked back at Sticky. He wasn't smiling anymore. Now his head was going side to side. Like he was shaking it, telling me no!

"Uh, never mind," I said to my dad. Then I eyed Sticky like, Was that what you wanted, boy?

His mouth curved back and then...he nodded.

I swear, he nodded!

My mom said, "Your dad was suggesting you catch him, Nolan. Before he runs away?"

I laughed. "He's not going anywhere." I turned back to Sticky. "Are you, boy?"

Sticky climbed up my collar.

He stuck his nose in my ear.

It tickled like crazy!

"Hey, hombre. What's up?"

What? Had Sticky just whispered in my ear?

All of a sudden, Sticky whipped around and sat on my shoulder backward. I looked around, and there was my dad, leaning in right behind me, grinning.

"Don't show your teeth, Dad! He'll think you want to eat him!"

"What I want," my mom said firmly, "is for you to catch him."

Dad reached up to do it, but like lightning, Sticky jumped off my shoulder! He zoomed across the floor! Up my wall! Across the ceiling! And that's where he stopped. Upside down, eight feet up, right in the middle of my ceiling.

Dad closed the door.

Mom put her hands on her hips and leaned her head way back. "What makes them able to *do* that?" she asked. "Suction cups?"

"Geometry!" I answered, looking up at the world's raddest reptile.

"Geometry?"

"Yeah! Their feet are covered with millions of little hairs that split into hundreds of even tinier hairs. Each of their feet has, like, a billion tiny hairs!"

"So what's that got to do with geometry?" my dad asked. He was moving a chair underneath Sticky.

"Yeah," my mom added. "Sounds like their feet need a hairstylist."

"Mo-om! It's the *angle* that the toe hairs contact the surface. And they can adjust the angle by curling and uncurling their toes." I pointed to the ceiling. "See him? He's getting a better grip right now."

Dad was up on the chair now, reaching for Sticky. Slowly, slowly, slowly his hand went up. But just as he was about to grab him, Sticky scampered away. Across the ceiling! Down the wall! Under my desk! Up my leg! Across my chest!

111

Around my neck! Then he perched right on my shoulder.

"Hiya, Sticky," I said. "Having fun?"

"Nolan," Mom whispered. "Catch him!"

"He's not going anywhere, are you, boy?"

Sticky grinned.

"Are you refusing to catch him, Nolan?" My mom was not sounding too friendly.

"He trusts me, Mom. If I try to catch him, he'll run off and never come back."

Mom looked at Dad.

Dad looked at Mom.

They had one of their silent conversations, and then Dad said, "So let's get you in the car."

I almost blurted, *Why?* but I knew why.

Sticky wasn't mine.

He was The Gecko's.

"What about dinner?" my mom asked.

"I think this is more important right now," my dad said. "It won't take long."

"Give me one minute, okay?" I wiggled my computer mouse to get rid of the screen saver and whispered to Sticky, "Check it out." I played the fire sprinkler clip for him, then whispered, "I'm sending this to people at newspapers and television stations all over the country. We're gonna put the Mole out of business. Cool, huh?"

Sticky was checking out the screen, watching my every move.

"All I have to do is click Send." I smiled at him. "Ready?"

Sticky's nose bobbed up and down.

"Okay, here goes!" I said, and with a click, *whoosh*, my message went zipping to computers all around the country!

Even across the world, to Timbuktu!

Dad nudged Mom with his elbow and cleared his throat. "You're not afraid Sticky there will tell people you're Shredderman?"

I blinked at him, then at Sticky.

Uh-oh.

Sticky was *grinning* at me.

"You won't, will you, boy?"

Sticky just kept on grinning.

What had I been *thinking*?

"It's top-secret!" I whispered to him. "Don't breathe a word of this to anyone, okay?"

Sticky's grin got bigger.

Uh-triple-oh!

People think I'm smart?

Ha! I'd just given away my secret identity to a hairy-toed klepto!

CHAPTER 14
The Boys Who Talk to Geckos

Mom stayed home to keep dinner warm while Dad and I headed back to Old Town. Dad called Henna Blockwell from the car to let her know we were coming, and Sticky stayed right on my shoulder the whole way. He loved looking out the window!

When we got to the Historian, Sticky ran off my shoulder and wiggled inside my sweatshirt. It tickled like crazy! Finally he turned around and peeked out over my zipper. I could feel his head going back and forth by my throat.

"Look!" my dad said as we walked through the front door. "There's Chase."

Chase ran over when he saw us and said, "You got him?"

I pointed to where I could feel Sticky hanging on my zipper. "He's right there."

"Yes!" Chase said. "Hey there, buddy. Steal anything while you were out?" He leveled his hand so it was right under my chin, then just held it there, waiting. "Come on. Let's go have some crickets!"

"Is that what they eat?" my dad asked.

"He loves 'em," Chase answered.

I could feel Sticky moving. Climbing. Then all at once, he jumped from my zipper, whipping me in the chin with his tail. He landed in Chase's hand, ran up his arm and around his neck, then perched on his shoulder.

"Welcome home, buddy," Chase said to him. Then, while Sticky was nosing around his neck and ear, he said to me, "Most people try to nab him." He laughed. "Good luck! But you handled him

right." He was about to say something more, only he stopped. He looked at Sticky. His eyes opened wide. "Is that so?" he said, then looked at me!

Uh-quadruple-oh!

"Is...is *what* so?" I asked.

Chase rubbed his chin.

His eyes sharpened down on me.

My heart was racing!

My knees were shaking!

I looked at Sticky, grinning away on his shoulder.

He told! Sticky told!

Then Chase nodded and said, "Sticky here seems to think you might be up for a game of Tekken 3."

My eyes and mouth felt frozen open. I couldn't blink! I couldn't quit gaping.

Tekken 3?

I checked Sticky. He was still grinning away.

Finally my dad rubbed my back and said, "I'm sorry, but my wife's keeping dinner warm for us. We really do have to go."

"That's cool," Chase said. Then he added, "You heard what happened tonight?"

"We were...on our way home," my dad said, "but yes, we heard about it."

Chase shook his head. "For a sleepy little town, there sure was a lot of action today. Between that buffoon kid and the sprinklers coming on, we are *way* behind schedule."

"Uh, what caused the sprinklers to go off, anyway?" my dad asked.

"They're not sure. It was crazy in here! People running and screaming and tearing around in circles. The hotel management says someone must've set it off, but no one saw anything."

I wanted to shout, How could you have missed him? It was the Mole! but I made myself stay quiet.

Chase gave Sticky a rub on his head. "Whatever, we're stuck here an extra day." He looked at my dad and said, "Sorry, no offense."

Dad laughed. "None taken."

Chase grinned at me. "Thanks for bringing Sticky back. I was really worried about him."

"Sure," I said, then added, "I think he stowed away in my backpack."

"Hey, that's Sticky for you." He turned to Sticky and said, "Huh, you little stinker?"

Sticky flicked out his tongue.

"See?" Chase said.

I laughed and said, "Yeah," and Dad seemed amused.

"Anyway," Chase said, "if you've got time, come back tomorrow. Maybe we can battle on a break or something."

"I'll try to come after school."

"Cool," he said, and turned to go, calling, "Thanks again!"

Sticky twisted around on Chase's shoulder so he was riding backward as they walked away. He was watching me!

And since he was *still* watching when they got to the elevator, I called, "Bye, Sticky!" and waved.

Then the coolest thing happened, and Dad saw it, too!

Sticky peeled up a hand...

And waved back.

CHAPTER 15
Scared Circuitless

The next morning, I almost pretended I was sick. I didn't want to go to school! Not because I wanted to fake it so I could go back to Old Town and play The Gecko in Tekken 3—I was planning to go there *after* school. No, I was afraid to go to school because I knew Bubba was going to pound me.

Or poison me!

Or at least corner me and fumigate me with Bubba-breath.

Pretending to be sick seemed a whole lot safer than being hospitalized!

But then my mom came in my room and said, "Good morning, honey! How's my superhero this morning?"

And that's when I knew I had to go to school.

Superheroes don't stay home sick! Even when they really are!

They go out there and take their licks.

And when they're down, they get right back up and try again!

What kind of superhero's afraid of Bubba-breath?

I tried to block out the thought of Bubba's fist. And his humongous size. And while I gobbled down my peanut-buttered Eggo, I let my mom kid me about Sticky. She hadn't believed a word of what I'd told her the night before, and since Dad was now calling Sticky's wave a "coincidence," I quit arguing.

I know what I saw!

So I just brushed my teeth, strapped on my backpack, and headed across the street.

That doesn't mean I hung around the playground waiting to be pounded, though.

No way!

I did my power-walk straight for my classroom. Bubba wouldn't touch me in front of the substitute! I could hang out there all day.

All week!

So I zoomed up the ramp and tried the door, but it was locked! I looked in the window, hoping Miss Newby was there.

She wasn't.

So I power-walked over to the computer lab.

Same story—locked up tight.

So was the library!

I started sweating bullets again. Where could I go? The minute Bubba spotted me, I'd be fried like a microchip in a power surge.

"Hi, Nolan," a voice behind me said.

My hair shot straight out!

My knees buckled underneath me!

I landed with a painful bump on the cement before I realized that it couldn't be Bubba. It was a *girl's* voice. And she'd said Nolan, not Nerd.

I looked up. Trinity Althoffer had her mouth covered with both hands. "I'm sorry!" she said. "I didn't mean to scare you!"

"That's okay," I said, trying to get up. I keep my backpack so loaded with things that it gets pretty heavy. And right now I was like a turtle stuck on its back.

She put out a hand to help me, and I almost didn't take it.

Superheroes don't need help from girls!

But she grabbed my arm and yanked, then asked, "Did you really meet The Gecko?"

Uh-oh.

"Where'd you...where'd you hear that?" I asked.

"Kevin and Max are going around telling everyone. They're saying Bubba saw you on the set. With a special visitor's badge and everything." She was still holding on to my arm, even though I was back on my feet. "Is it true?"

"Uh...well...um...maybe."

"*Maybe?* How can it *maybe* be true?"

My circuits were overloaded. I couldn't think of what to say! What to do! I looked over both shoulders like crazy. "I...uh...I was just there with my dad."

"Because he's a reporter, right?"

"Uh-huh."

"That's great! Tell me all about it!"

I wished she would just leave me alone. "Have you seen Bubba?"

"We're supposed to call him Alvin, remember?"

"Yeah, if you like getting pounded!"

"Nolan!" she said with a scowl. "I call him Alvin all the time. Do I look pounded?"

She did? Why hadn't I ever heard her do that? "No...," I said. "But you're a, you know, *girl*."

She punched me in the arm. "So what?"

"Hey!" Boy, for a girl who spent her life drawing ponies, she sure punched hard!

"And yeah, I saw him," she added. "Down by the swings. Now tell me about being on the set!"

The warning bell rang, and I let out a huge sigh of relief. The substitute would unlock the room in no time! Safety was a power-walk away!

Trinity followed me as I zoomed along the walkway. "Why don't you want to talk about it?" she asked. "Did something happen? Did you trip or fall or something? Did they kick you off the set?"

My head whipped around to face her. "No, I didn't trip! And stop making fun of me!"

"I'm not making fun of you," she said. "I'm just, you know, wondering."

"Well, *I'm* not the one who got kicked off the set," I snapped.

She raced along beside me. "But...you're saying...you're saying someone *did?*"

All of a sudden, there was Bubba. Looming large and deadly across the blacktop. He was looking at me, too. And coming my way!

This was it, I could tell. In a few seconds, I'd be nothing but nerd nuggets.

But then the strangest thing happened.

Bubba turned.

No push.

No punch.

No threat.

No *breath.*

He just went into the classroom.

"Wow," Trinity whispered. "He looks really different."

He still looked plenty mean to me.

And totally deadly.

But she was right. Something was different. I tried to figure out what. It wasn't his clothes or his hair or his—

"He looks . . . *depressed*," she said.

It was the weirdest thing since quantum dots, but yes, that was it exactly.

We waited a minute before going up the ramp into the classroom. Neither of us could quite believe it.

Bubba Bixby depressed?

Inside the classroom, the air felt totally dead. Like the room was in a vacuum. Eyes were shifting around uneasily, but no one was talking. Even Miss Newby seemed to understand that something strange was going on. She just stood behind the teacher desk, looking at all of us looking at each other.

"Good morning, class," she finally said.

"Good morning," a few of us mumbled.

Then she did something only a substitute would be crazy enough to do. She asked, "Is everything all right, Alvin?"

His face was leaning on one beefy hand. He shrugged. And scowled.

He looked like a monster with a toothache.

"Alvin?" she asked again.

"What!" he snapped at her.

She jerked back a little, then took a deep breath and said, "Would you like to—"

"What? Go to the office?" He was looking a lot like that grizzly bear at the Historian.

"No!" he growled. "Just leave me alone."

"But if you—"

"I said no!"

Everyone held their breath, including Miss Newby. Then very slowly, Bubba looked over his shoulder, right at me. "Why don't you kick *him* out?" he grumbled.

All heads in class turned until everyone was staring at me. I shrank lower in my seat. I wanted to hide! And Miss Newby was about to ask *me* something, but Trinity stood up like she was giving an oral report and said, "Alvin's upset because Nolan got to meet The Gecko."

"The . . . Gecko?" Miss Newby asked.

"Shut up, Pony-girl!" Bubba snapped.

"Alvin!" Miss Newby scolded.

"Well, it's none of her stupid business!" Bubba shouted.

Miss Newby said, "Please, Alvin. Control yourself!"

Uh-triple-oh! If you know anything about Bubba Bixby, you know that that was the complete wrong thing to say to him. And sure enough, he stood up, threw his chair over, and stomped out of the room.

But not before giving me the deadliest glare I'd ever seen.

Miss Newby picked up the classroom phone and called the office. And after whispering like mad for a minute, she hung up, straightened Bubba's chair, and tried to smile. "Well, class. It seems we're off to a bumpy start this morning." Then she just stood there with a twitchy smile, trying to figure out what she should do next.

Trinity whispered, "Wow. He looked like he was about to cry!"

"Cry?" I said. "He looked like he was about to *kill* me!"

"Yeah, but I'm talking about underneath all that." She turned to Freddy, next to her. "Didn't you think he looked like he was going to cry?"

Freddy scowled at her. "Bubba? Cry? You're psycho, Pony-girl."

She punched him in the arm. "Don't call me psycho *or* Pony-girl, Pee-boy!"

He turned beet red and shut up.

It felt like none of us would survive the day.

CHAPTER 16
Crazy Idea

Miss Newby finally gave us a reading assignment. "Take out your social studies book. Read pages one-forty-two through one-fifty-two. When you're done, answer questions one through eleven on page one-fifty-three."

We all pulled our books out and started reading.

It had never been so quiet in Room 22.

Social studies is not my favorite subject to begin with. It usually feels like I'm feeding my brain sawdust. So somewhere in the middle of reading about the people of Brazil, I started daydreaming. For once I wasn't daydreaming about an invention or playing on my computer. Or being Shredderman. Or watching *The Gecko and Sticky*.

I was thinking about Bubba.

And about Bubba's dad. I've seen Mr. Bixby in action, and boy! He's just like Bubba, only bigger.

And meaner.

I was also thinking about my dad. My totally great dad, who calls me champ, and helps me be Shredderman, and took me to meet The Gecko.

How could two dads be so different?

How could two kids be so different?

What if I had to live with Bubba's dad? Would I get meaner?

What if Bubba got to live with my dad? Would he get nicer?

Was *that* the key to making Bubba nicer?

Was there even a key? Or was Bubba always going to be the same?

I think the rest of the kids in class were daydreaming, too, because everybody jumped when Dr. Voss walked in the room.

Dr. Voss is our principal, and her walking in a

room can make you jump all by itself, but now she wasn't alone. She had Bubba with her.

Everybody pretended to be reading, but eyes were shifting around like crazy!

Bubba didn't look at anything but the ground, and went straight to his seat while Dr. Voss and Miss Newby stood off to one side and whispered.

And even though Bubba didn't look at anyone, everyone in class noticed—Bubba's eyes were red and puffy.

All the kids in class twitched their faces and mouths. They were spreading the word without saying a word.

Bubba Bixby had been crying!

Crying.

For the rest of school, no one knew what to do. Or say. Even Kevin and Max steered clear of him. And although Bubba was quieter than he'd ever been, something about him looked extra angry.

Extra dangerous.

So, believe me, I was shaking in my shoes! But at recess, nothing happened. And at lunch, instead of stalking kids like a tower of terror, Bubba sat by himself on the lower field, throwing pebbles at the grass.

All kinds of kids asked me about meeting The Gecko, and normally talking about it would have been great. But I didn't want to talk about it. It felt like showing off your Christmas presents when the guy next to you only got a lump of coal.

Even if the guy next to you *deserved* a lump of coal, it still felt...wrong.

Besides, a lot of kids were telling me I was history. Toast. Nothing but walking worm food.

And I had the feeling that they were right. Bubba hated me so bad now, he was probably planning something even wickeder than usual. My stomach was in knots! My throat choked off! I couldn't even remember my times tables!

Then during math, I got the world's craziest

idea. I actually dropped my pencil, it was that crazy. But the more I thought about it, the more sense it made. The more I wanted to do it.

It would either change things, or get me killed.

I just had to get up enough nerve to find out which.

CHAPTER 17

Alvin Emerges

When school let out, I followed Bubba to the bike racks.

My heart was beating like crazy!

I got on the other side of the racks, looked right at him, and said, "I can take you to meet The Gecko."

He stopped pulling his bike back. "What?"

I cleared my throat. "I said, I can take you to meet The Gecko."

He squinted at me, then snorted and yanked his bike the rest of the way out of the rack. "Quit pulling my chain, Nerd."

I followed him as he headed for the street. "I'm

serious. He said I could come back today. I'll take you with me."

Bubba stopped and looked at me like I ate flies. Finally he said, *"Why?"*

I shrugged. "Because...I'd like to?"

"Shut up, Nerd. You expect me to believe that?"

"I'm serious! I'll go get my bike. We can ride over to Old Town together."

He just stared at me.

"Wait here," I told him. "I'll be right back!"

I tore home, told Mom where I was going, jumped on my bike, and raced back to school.

Bubba was still there.

"Come on!" I shouted as I coasted past him. "Let's go!"

Bubba Bixby may be big and mean, full of teeth and ready to bite, but he's not very fast on a bike. I had to stop and wait for him at least three times!

And the whole way there, he didn't say one word to me.

Not one.

We parked our bikes at a rack in front of Old Town, and when we were walking over to the hotel, I told him, "They're probably going to recognize you from yesterday, so just let me handle it, okay?"

He nodded. His cheeks were like McIntosh apples, and he was dripping sweat.

He still didn't say a word.

At the hotel, we got stopped by a security guard. I told him, "The Gecko…uh…Chase Morton invited us."

"Oh, right," he said sarcastically. He squinted at Bubba, saying, "Didn't I specifically invite you to *not* come back?"

Bubba looked down.

So I said, "He's here with me today. I'm Nolan Byrd. Ask Chase. He'll tell you it's all right."

"Hmmm," the guard said.

"Or Henna Blockwell. She knows it's okay."

He studied me a minute, then got on his walkie-talkie radio. Five minutes later, Henna showed up and let us in. "Hi, Nolan. Chase told me if you showed up to send you upstairs. Apparently he's got some new move to wipe you out in Tekken 3." She looked at her watch and said, "He's only got about ten minutes before his call time." Then she noticed that Bubba was following along.

"Uh...Nolan?" she whispered. "Isn't he the boy who ruined the take yesterday?"

I nodded.

"I don't think we can—"

"Please, Miss Blockwell? It's...it's kind of hard to explain, but it's important. And if we've only got ten minutes..." I shrugged. "Please?"

She looked from me to Bubba and back again. Finally she sighed and said, "Well, come along."

Chase was sitting cross-legged on his bed. His thumbs were flying on his PlayStation controller. "Nolan!" he said when he saw me. "My man!" He tossed me the second controller. "I am gonna wipe you out!"

We entered a battle. I was Yoshimitsu Green. He was Yoshimitsu Red. He had totally mastered backflips. And the deathcopter trick! And samurai cutter! He was even using slap-u-silly!

Whoa!

But I managed to slash and bash and dance all around him. It was close, but I won the round!

"How'd you *do* that?" Chase cried.

"Man," Bubba mumbled. "You're good."

"Huh?" Chase said, finally noticing Bubba. "Hey…" He squinted at him. "How'd *you* get in here?"

"I, um, I brought him," I said.

"You're *friends* with that guy?" Chase asked, his eyebrows flying up.

"Well, um..." I looked at Bubba. "Not exactly."

"So...?" Chase was starting to look annoyed. Maybe even mad.

"I... I brought him because I thought it was... a nice thing to do." I looked down and said, "It's a long story, and really complicated. Don't be mad, okay?"

"Okaaaaaay," Chase said, studying me. Then he nodded and stuck out his hand to Bubba. "I'm Chase Morton." He wiggled his eyebrows. "The Gecko!"

Bubba shook his hand. "I'm... Bub...," he said, then stopped himself. "I'm... Alvin Bixby." He started pumping Chase's hand like crazy. "Your number one fan!"

"Well, hey, Alvin. Nice to *officially* meet you." Then Chase eyed me and asked him, "You think your friend here will let me whip you in Tekken 3?"

I looked at Bubba.

Bubba looked at me.

And it was weird. He didn't even seem like Bubba.

He seemed more like an oversized toddler.

I held out the controller to him and grinned. "Go easy on him. He's just a superhero."

Bubba laughed and took my place on the bed. "You gonna be Yoshimitsu again?" he asked Chase.

"You bet! You?"

"Nah," Bubba said. "I choose True Ogre! He's rad!"

"Hoo-hoo-hoo!" Chase laughed.

And the battle began.

CHAPTER 18

Out of Control!

Yoshimitsu clobbered True Ogre. What do you expect when a gargoyle with flame-breath takes on a Manji ninja? But Bubba didn't even seem to care. He said, "You want to go again?"

Chase would have, but Henna came in and made them stop. So Chase made Henna get Bubba a poster that Chase autographed and signed: *To Alvin "Bubba" Bixby, who rocks at Tekken 3.* And since no visitors were being allowed on the set, we had to leave the building, but not before I took a quick picture of Bubba and Chase with my digital camera.

When we were unlocking our bikes, I asked Bubba, "You got e-mail?"

Like I didn't know!

Then I added, "I'll download the picture of you and The Gecko and send it to you."

He frowned for a minute, then said, "Bixby at BigNet-dot-com." He pulled his bike from the rack and stared at me. For a guy who had just met The Gecko, he sure wasn't looking too friendly.

He stood there for a minute like he was trying to figure out how to say something, but it never came out. And finally he just swung onto his bike and left. No *See ya*, no wave. He just took off.

So I took off, too, only I went a different way. And I wondered what Bubba had been trying to say.

Thanks?

Nah, more likely it was *Don't think this makes us friends, Nerd!*

Like I would want to be!

Or *Don't start thinking you can e-mail me, Geek.*

Too late for that. I'd been e-mailing him for months!

As Shredderman!

So I was thinking about how I'd have to use my parents' e-mail system to mail Bubba the picture, but the minute I got home, I forgot all about Bubba. My mom was screaming, "Nolan! Nolan, come here quick!"

I dropped my backpack and charged for the kitchen. "Mom? What's wrong? Mom?"

"In here!" she yelled from the family room. "*Look.*"

Her eyes were cranked open.

Her jaw was dropped to the floor.

She was tearing apart her purse trying to find her phone, but she wasn't looking at what she was doing.

She was looking at the TV.

"What's wrong, Mom? What's..." And then I heard a voice from the television say, "...Shredderman."

Two newscasters were talking about *me* on TV!

"It's everywhere," the man was saying to the lady next to him. "I got the e-mail this morning, you got it last night. Everyone in the industry seems to have a copy of Joel Bowl vandalizing that hotel"—he shuffled through some papers—"the Historian up in Cedar Valley."

The lady was nodding. "And I've heard the hotel *and* the production company are planning to press charges."

"So this might be the Mole's last digging spree?" the man asked.

"I, for one, hope so!" The lady grinned into the camera and said, "Meanwhile, good work, Shredderman, whoever you are."

"Yeah," the man added. "What's that motto of his?"

"Yours in truth and justice!"

"Exactly!" The man turned to the camera and said, "And now to Bill McCloud, who hopefully has some truth and justice to convey to us about the weather...."

Mom had found her cell phone. She muted the TV while she pressed buttons on her phone with her thumb. "That was news out of Los Angeles!" she whispered to me. Then she said into the phone, "Steven? Steven, you are never

going to believe what was just on Channel Five...."

Wow. If it had been on Los Angeles TV, where else had it been? I charged down to my room to check my e-mail. While I'd been worried about surviving a day at school, stuff had been happening! People had been talking! Sending my clip around! Cedar Valley and the Historian had been on big-city news!

I booted up.

Dialed up the Internet.

Checked my mail.

Flick...flick...flick, e-mails sprang up from the bottom of my in-box!

Flick...flick...flick-flick-flick!

Flick-flick-flick-flick-flick-flick-flick!

My screen was going crazy! Messages were flying in! Scrolling off the screen faster than I could read who they were from!

I watched them for a whole minute.

Two!

I got out of my chair and backed up.

Whoa! They were *still* flying in!

Finally I clicked on Send and Receive, and there was the blue line, only partway done. And the message said, **Receiving... 302 out of 927 messages**.

927 messages?

303, 304, 305, 306... The ones column was spinning around like the cents counter at the gas pump!

Who were all these people?

Mom wandered into my room without knocking.

That happens when you leave your door wide open.

She still had her phone attached to her ear. She was making little sounds into it. Fragmented sentences. Nuh-uhs and Uh-huhs. Sighs and tisking noises.

Then all of a sudden, she gasped like she'd spotted a Tyrannosaurus rex in my room.

I jumped and looked around.

No T. rex. *Phew.*

"He's got nine hundred twenty-seven messages!" she whispered into the phone. "Steven, this is totally out of control!" Her eyes were enormous. "Uh-huh. Okay. All right. I don't know, okay? Uh-huh. All right. Call back when you can." She flipped the phone closed and sat on the edge of my bed. "Nolan? Your dad won't be home for a while."

"Uh-huh." I was scrolling through messages. Dad worked late a lot.

"The *Gazette*'s been flooded with calls about Shredderman."

I looked at her. "Really?"

"And since your father is supposedly spearheading the investigation into who Shredderman is, he's having to steer people in the wrong direction."

I grinned at her. "Cool!"

"Cool?"

"Yeah! It's great that Dad can help out like that."

"But—"

"He's turning out to be a pretty good sidekick, huh?"

"Sidekick? Nolan, he's your father!"

"Who's being a pretty good sidekick!" I was still grinning. My dad as a sidekick. Something about the idea seemed really...cool.

"Mr. Green's your sidekick, remember?" She was looking a little miffed.

"But Mr. Green's in Oregon. And Dad's been real helpful, you know?"

"But—"

"Call him a substitute sidekick, if you want."

"I don't want to call him *any* kind of sidekick! He's a reporter and he's not supposed to lie or cover up or—" Her cell phone rang, interrupting her. She flipped it open. "Yes?"

I was busy racing through messages. People loved Shredderman!

She listened, then whispered, "CNN? What did you tell them?"

CNN? National news? That got my attention!

"Tonight?" she was saying. "Wow, they work fast. Okay. Yes, I will. No, no, don't worry. I'm keeping him right here." She was about to hang up, but at the last minute asked, "Hey—what are your thoughts on being called a substitute sidekick?"

She laughed and rolled her eyes, then hung up.

"What did he say?" I asked.

"He said, 'Cool!'"

"Well, no matter, let's come to know the author. He, she, they, I'm intrigued..."

"Introduction to our former president's new..." "...that guy who..."

"...how she brought together Indy with the back and her hand. It's the same ride, beautiful ride... Roberto, I mean, said..."

CHAPTER 19
National News

That night they talked about Shredderman on CNN, ABC, CBS, and Fox News. And in the morning we ate breakfast and listened while a group of morning-show anchors talked about it over coffee. "He sounds like some kind of vigilante," one of the guys was saying.

"No, he's not," the blond lady said. "I think he's just a kid. Did you check out his Web site?"

"He's got a Web site?" the guy asked.

"Shredderman-dot-com," she said. "It's a hoot. Intelligent, but also very kidlike."

"I think it's a teacher," the other guy said. "No kid could possibly put a site like that together."

"Well, no teacher's going to have a link called Bubba's Big Butt," the lady said.

"There's a link to our former president's butt?" the first guy asked.

"No!" she laughed, tagging him with the back of her hand. "It's just some kid's backside. Fully covered, I might add."

"So maybe the teacher's got it in for a trouble-maker."

"Maybe Shredderman *is* the troublemaker."

"No! How can you say that after he busted Joel the Mole? Shredderman's a champion of truth and justice."

"Well, speaking of truth and justice," the first guy said, "we were talking about lobbyists, remember?"

"Right!" The lady looked in the camera and said, "And we want to hear what *you* think should be done about special-interest groups. Give us a call or log on to—"

Mom clicked off the TV and muttered, "I told you we should take Bubba's Big Butt off the World Wide Web!"

"It'll blow over," Dad said. "Tomorrow they'll have forgotten all about Shredderman." He winked at me as he stood up and grabbed his coat. "Today, though, I'm probably going to have to spend a lot of time trying to mislead people about our town's superhero."

"Thanks, Dad," I told him.

He smiled. "No problem, champ." He nodded at the kitchen clock. "You'd better get moving if you don't want to be late for school."

Yikes! How'd that happen? There were only fifteen minutes before the opening bell rang!

I tore down the hall to get dressed. Socks *inside* pants—check!

I raced down to the bathroom to brush my teeth.

No time to floss! My hair was sticking out everywhere!

I tried spraying it
down.

Boing! It shot right
back up.

I stuck my head in
the sink. No time to
mess around!

"Uh, Nolan?" My
mom's arm was poking
through the bathroom door.
She was holding out the phone
to me. "It's Mr. Green."

Mr. Green?

I took the phone. "Hello?" Water was dripping
everywhere!

"Hey, Nolan. Just calling to say congratula-
tions. According to my TV, you're making some
pretty big waves out there."

"Thanks, Mr. Green," I said. Then I whispered,
"You haven't told anyone it's me...have you?"

He laughed. "Of course not. I'm just sorry I'm missing all the action. But it sounds like you're doing just fine without me."

"Well, my dad's helping out. I'm calling him my substitute sidekick!"

Mr. Green laughed. "That's great. And speaking of substitutes, how's Miss Newby holding up?"

"Okay, I guess. How's your brother doing?"

"Great! We're calling him Bionic Boy. I should be back next week."

"Really?"

"Uh-huh. I'll see you then. Meanwhile, keep up the good work!"

"Thanks, Mr. Green."

"Now get a move on or you're going to be tardy!"

"Right!" I said, and hung up.

Ready or not, it was time for school.

CHAPTER 20
Bye-bye, Big Butt

By the time I got to school, there was a big crowd of kids gathered on the playground.

Not one ball was bouncing on the blacktop!

I worked my way through the crowd until I could see what was going on. And then I saw him, smack-dab in the middle of everybody.

Bubba.

"Stand back!" Kevin and Max were telling kids. "Nobody touches it!"

"Is it for real?" Ian asked.

"Yeah, it's for real!" Bubba said. "You think I could *fake* this?" He was holding up his autographed poster, careful to only handle the edges.

"How'd you *get* it?" Trinity asked. "I can't

believe you actually *met* Chase Morton! That is so, so cool!"

"Yeah!" everyone said. "How'd you meet him?"

"He has his ways," Kevin said, like he was the smartest kid around. "Now back up! Quit crowding!"

"Aw, it's a fake," someone from the back yelled. "There's no way that's real!"

"Shut up, stupid!" Bubba yelled back. "It's a hundred percent authentic!"

"Oh, right," the voice snickered.

"Who's sayin' that?" Bubba asked. "I want to know who's sayin' that!"

Max started pushing through the crowd, saying, "All right, who's the smart mouth?"

"Hey!" I called. "Don't fight! Bubba really did meet The Gecko. I... I've got proof!"

"Huh?" everyone said, then turned to look at me.

Kevin sneered, "*You?*"

I called over to Bubba, "I've got a copy right here. Do you want it?"

Bubba kind of bit his lip, then looked down and nodded.

Everyone started whispering.

So I peeled off my backpack and pulled out a big envelope.

The whispering stopped.

Everyone crowded in.

"Back up!" Bubba growled. "Now!"

Kids scurried back, and I said, "I, uh...I couldn't get online last night...." I stepped closer and handed over the envelope. "So I made you this."

Bubba took the envelope.

He opened it.

Then he broke into a smile and held the picture of him and The Gecko up high. "See?" he said. "Proof!"

Everyone ooooohed.

They aaaaahed!

Then Kevin piped up with, "Wait a minute.
The *Nerd* took that? What was *he* doing there?"

The ooooohing and aaaaahing stopped.

Kids looked at Bubba.

At me!

At Bubba!

At me!

And finally Bubba cleared his throat and said, "Nolan's the one who got me in to see The Gecko."

"*Who* did?" a lot of kids asked.

Bubba nodded my way. "Nolan did. He got me inside. Introduced me. Even let me play The Gecko in Tekken 3. He was ... he was really cool."

Mouths were gasping.

Eyes were bugging!

Nobody could believe their ears!

Especially Kevin. He squinted at Bubba and said, "Wait a minute. You're saying the Nerd—"

"I'm saying *Nolan*," Bubba said, giving him a deep, dark glare, "did me a big favor, okay?"

"O ... kaaaaay," Kevin said, and backed off.

For the rest of the day, people treated me ...

differently. They weren't trying to be my best friends or anything, but people wanted to know.

About meeting The Gecko.

About playing him in Tekken 3.

About taking Bubba to meet him, too.

After everything Bubba had done to me—all the names he'd called me and the punches he'd thrown at me and the stuff he'd stolen from me—they just didn't get why I'd done it.

I didn't explain it. How could I explain that the search for truth and justice wasn't just about getting even? It was about being bigger than yourself. Stronger than your weaknesses.

So I just shrugged and told them, "Because he really wanted to meet him, that's why."

Later that day, I thought about what Mr. Green had said about finding the key to Bubba's kindness. Maybe after everything I'd tried, this was finally it.

Not that I expected Bubba to become Mr. Nice

Guy. He'd probably always be more like True Ogre than Yoshimitsu.

But this *was* a start. A good start.

So after school I went home and did something I never thought I'd be able to do.

I took **Bubba's Big Butt** off the World Wide Web.

I'll be okay without it.

Plus, it leaves more room to shred on the next guy who tries to mess around with truth and justice.

Oh, yeah!

CHAPTER 21
E-mail #2,543

Hey, Shredderman,

Rumor is the Mole's out of business. Blacklisted. You rock, man.

Your #1 fan,
Chase Morton

P.S. I told myself it couldn't be you, but Sticky says it's true. No wonder I couldn't beat you in T-3. I was battling a real, live superhero! Shred on, man!

P.P.S. (Don't worry—no one suspects, and I won't tell.)